LONGBOARD
Letdown

BY JAKE MADDOX

text by Cari Meister
illustrated by Katie Wood

STONE ARCH BOOKS
a capstone imprint

Jake Maddox Books are published by Stone Arch Books
a Capstone imprint
1710 Roe Crest Drive
North Mankato, Minnesota 56003
www.mycapstone.com

Library of Congress Cataloging-in-Publication data is available on the
Library of Congress website.

978-1-4965-4972-3 (library binding) — 978-1-4965-4974-7 (paperback) —
978-1-4965-4976-1 (eBook PDF)

Summary: Valeria has always been one of the best downhill longboarders
around, but as she comes back from an injury, she seems to have lost her
fearlessness. The annual longboarding race is right around the corner and
Valeria has always dominated the locals kids division. Everyone expects this
year to be the same — everyone except Valeria.

Designer: Sarah Bennett
Production Specialist: Tori Abraham

Artistic Elements: Shutterstock

Printed in Canada.
010382F17

J
MADDOX
JAKE

A Spanish phrase guide can be found on page 65.

TABLE OF CONTENTS

Chapter One

REPLAY

Valeria Pérez stuck her pencil down her cast and scratched. *Just a little farther,* she thought. *There! Ahh. Much better.*

Mateo kicked her chair. "Don't you get that off soon?" he asked.

Valeria turned around and flashed her best friend a smile. "Today!" she said.

"*Chido!*" said Mateo. "Can you meet me at the skate park later?"

Valeria stared out the window.

"Valeria? Hello?" Mateo said, waving.

Mr. Rudder, their sixth-grade English teacher, looked up and cleared his throat.

"Valeria. Mateo. Are you finished with your journal entries?" he asked.

Yeah right, Valeria thought. Writing with her cast on was so slow!

Her thoughts drifted to the longboard crash. Ever since crashing six weeks ago, she had replayed the accident over and over. She couldn't stop thinking about it. Of course this was a bad mindset, but she couldn't help it.

BEEP! Class was over.

"So," Mateo pressed, "when are you gonna check out my turns? I want to make sure I'm ready for the comp this weekend."

He was talking about the longboarding race — the "comp," short for "competition."

Before Valeria could answer, Mateo kept talking. "Did you hear? The comp's on Brayon Gulch now. It'll be steeper and more difficult than High Valley."

Valeria hadn't heard. She had only ridden Brayon Gulch Road once. Usually there was too much traffic. She remembered one really steep downhill section and a few long, steady parts.

High Valley was where the comp had been the last two years. Valeria had won the U14 (under fourteen) girls division both times. It was fun, but not nearly as thrilling as Brayon Gulch Road.

Mateo sat on her desk. "So?" he said. "Can you make it later?"

Valeria shoved her books into her backpack and zipped it shut.

"I don't know," she said. "I'll try."

Chapter Two

PANIC

Valeria headed to the free clinic after school. She was supposed to meet her mom, Coco, at 4:15. The clinic got really busy after five as people got off from work.

Valeria got there at 4:10. She went in and saw Lido, an older girl from her trailer park, at the reception desk.

"Hey, Lido. I didn't know you worked here," said Valeria.

"I just started." said Lido. "Basically I make copies and translate for Dr. Pauly."

This made sense. There were lots of Mexican people in Harlow Springs. Some only spoke Spanish. Valeria, like many of her friends, had been born in Colorado. Her parents had come from Mexico.

"Are you here for your cast?" Lido asked.

Valeria nodded. "My mom is coming."

Valeria sat down in a worn pink chair and looked at the clock. 4:20. Her mom was late. This wasn't surprising. She was the head housekeeper at a local resort hotel. If one of the other housekeepers called in sick, Coco had to clean extra rooms.

Sitting there, Valeria began to feel stressed. She imagined going to school tomorrow with no cast. Everyone would think she was dying to longboard again. But no one knew she was scared to ride. The whole situation made her mad.

Why am I so scared? she thought. *I used to love the speed of boarding down a hill, even when it felt a little dangerous! Longboarding's been my passion for four years. I've never gotten hurt before. Now one injury's going to stop me?*

At 4:45, Coco finally rushed in. Valeria was chewing her nails, wondering if she could get Dr. Pauly to leave her cast on.

Coco bent down and kissed Valeria. "I'm sorry, *mi gatita*. It was crazy at work!"

"It's okay," said Valeria. "Maybe we should come back next week. I have a lot of homework. This could take a long time."

Just then a nurse called her name.

"Don't be silly," said Coco. "I'm sure it won't take long!"

* * *

The next morning, Mateo ran to catch up with Valeria. "Let me see!" he said.

Valeria held up her arm. It looked weird and thin after being in the cast.

"Sweet!" said Mateo. "You're healed!"

Valeria nodded. "But I have to wear a Velcro support when I board, just in case."

"*Chido*! I can't wait —" Mateo looked around Valeria. "Where's your board?"

"Sorry, Mateo. I told Señora Cruz I'd help at her daycare after school," Valeria lied.

"How about after dinner?" asked Mateo.

"I can't tonight," said Valeria.

"Tomorrow, then," said Mateo. "Okay?"

"Yeah, sure," said Valeria as she closed her locker. But she was already thinking of more excuses.

Chapter Three

THE NEW GIRL

Mateo was sitting in his usual spot at lunch. There was a new girl next to him.

"Valeria," Mateo said. "This is Chloe Platter. She just moved here."

"Hi," said Valeria as she sat down. "Where'd you move from?"

"Minneapolis," said Chloe.

"It's cold there, huh?" asked Valeria.

"Yeah. You walk outside and your nostril hairs freeze instantly," Chloe said as she made a goofy face.

Valeria and Mateo laughed.

"Chloe wants to learn to longboard," said Mateo. "I told her she should hang with you — 'cause you're the best."

Used to be, maybe, Valeria thought. *But now . . .*

"Yeah," said Chloe, "I figured you could show me how to break my arm. I've never done that and, hey, I need some attention. After all, I'm the new girl. I have to stand out in some way, right?" Then Chloe smiled at Valeria. "No seriously," she said. "Mateo told me how you won all the local comps."

Valeria smiled limply.

Chloe went on. "I've never even stood on a board, but it looks fun. Plus, my mother will freak out — and I'm still mad at her for moving here. So what do you say? Did I make you feel sorry for me yet?" Chloe sighed and made a pathetic face.

"If not here's a little more: I'm adopted," she said. "That usually makes people feel sorry for me. You know. Poor baby, abandoned by her parents."

Mateo and Valeria stared at Chloe, but then Chloe laughed. "Gotcha! See? It works! Now you can't say no, right?"

"Do you have a board?" asked Valeria.

"Not yet," said Chloe. "Mateo said he'd take me to Keep On Skating after school."

"My brother, Emilio, works there," said Valeria. "But I don't think they have any used downhill boards right now."

"But they sell new stuff too, right?" asked Chloe.

Valeria's eyes widened. A new setup — deck, wheels, trucks, grip tape — would be expensive. Valeria had to scrimp and save for a long time just to buy a set of wheels.

Chloe must have guessed what Valeria was thinking. "My grandparents gave me a wad of cash for my birthday," she said. "I'm their only grandchild. They tend to spoil me." Then she shrugged. "Hey, if I don't like longboarding, you can have the stuff I buy."

Chapter Four

BACK ON BOARD

The next morning Valeria had a sinking feeling. *How am I going to teach Chloe if I'm too scared to step on my board?* she thought. She was thinking about playing sick when Emilio knocked on her open door.

"Hey, *gatita*," Emilio said. "Mateo just texted me. He wants to make sure you bring your board to school."

"Got it," said Valeria, rolling over and covering her face.

She didn't know how to tell Emilio about her fear. She'd always been brave. Emilio was the one who got her on a board when she was only six. He was her biggest supporter. Once, he had even told her, "You could be a pro someday!"

Valeria forced herself out of bed. On her way out the door, Emilio shouted, "Don't forget to sign up for the comp — registration closes Saturday!"

* * *

After school, Valeria carried her well-loved board over to the parking lot. Mateo and Chloe were waiting for her.

Chloe had a new setup: a stiff downhill board with red grip tape and bright graphics on the underside, Butterball wheels, and drop-through mounted trucks.

Chloe was also wearing standard protective gear — helmet, slide gloves, kneepads, and elbow pads.

"Nice board," said Valeria.

"Thanks," said Chloe. "Your brother and Mateo helped me put it together.

"How about all my safety gear?" Chloe rolled her eyes. "Mother's rules. At least I talked her out of the hockey face mask."

Valeria laughed. "Hockey mask?"

"I told her no one would hang with me if I wore it — then I started crying about moving," Chloe said.

Valeria liked Chloe. She was funny.

Chloe bowed. "Okay, master," she said. "I'm ready for lesson one."

"So are you goofy foot or regular?" Valeria asked.

"Huh? Well, I guess my feet are regular," said Chloe. "I mean, I don't have any extra toes or anything. At least not anymore. I did have an extra toe, but they removed it. Does that make me regular or goofy?"

"Hold up," said Mateo. "Extra toe?"

Chloe nodded. "My mom thought it would make buying shoes hard, which I guess is true. But, if I still had it, I could wear sandals and freak people out, right?"

"Here," said Valeria, trying to contain her laughter. She held out her hands and helped Chloe get on the board. "Let's see if you're goofy or regular."

Chloe stepped on the board. "Whoa!" she said. "It really rolls."

"Don't worry," said Valeria. "I've got you. So, if you were going that way," Valeria pointed, "which foot would you lead with?"

Chloe shrugged. "I don't know."

"Okay," said Valeria. "We'll try it this way. Lie down on the ground."

Chloe did.

"Now get up," Valeria instructed.

Chloe got up, using her left foot first.

"You're goofy-footed," said Valeria, "like me. That means you will want your left foot forward on your board."

Valeria stepped on her board to show Chloe. "Let's just ride around the parking lot," said Valeria.

Chloe started to move, but she was standing too tall and lost her balance.

"Scrunch down like this," said Valeria, showing her. "The lower your center of gravity, the steadier you'll feel."

Chloe caught on fast. In the next hour, she had learned how to foot brake and turn.

"I think we can try the small hill by our houses tomorrow," Mateo said.

"Really?" said Chloe. "Are you sure?"

Mateo nodded.

Valeria thought for a moment. Riding on the flats was one thing, but downhill, that was something else. Valeria brushed the feeling aside. "Yeah," she said. "Let's do it. Hey, do you guys live by each other?"

"Chloe lives two streets up," said Mateo.

"652 Sugarbush Lane," said Chloe.

Chapter Five

CHLOE'S PLACE

"I guess this is it," Valeria said, looking up at the huge house. The style was similar to Mateo's — but Chloe's was about five times bigger. Before she could knock, Chloe came to the door. Mateo was already there.

"Hey," she said. "I'm almost ready."

A woman stood on the rug waiting for an introduction.

"Mother," Chloe said. "This is Valeria."

"Hello, I'm Mrs. Platter," Chloe's mom said. "Nice to meet you, Valeria. I hope you and Mateo will keep Chloe safe. I'm not sure longboarding is the right sport for her. Do either of you play tennis?"

"Mother!" said Chloe. "We have to go!"

"How about a snack?" Mrs. Platter asked.

"No, thank you," said Valeria. "I have to catch the 5:40 bus."

Mrs. Platter look confused. "Chloe said you lived close by."

"Mateo lives close —" Chloe looked at Valeria. "Where do you live?" she asked.

"The trailer park by Highway Nine," said Valeria. She wasn't sure how the Platters would take that. Sometimes people looked at her differently after they found out where she lived.

"The one across from the gardening shop?" Mrs. Platter asked.

Valeria nodded.

Mrs. Platter smiled. "I know just where that is. Okay, well, have fun — and *please* be careful with Chloe. She's the only daughter I've got!"

"Don't worry," said Mateo. "Valeria is the best teacher."

"And besides," said Valeria, "Chloe has plenty of safety gear!"

"Oh, that reminds me," said Mrs. Platter, "Chloe, you need your hockey mask. I think it's in the garage. Wait here. I'll get it."

"Mother!" said Chloe.

Mrs. Platter sighed and said, "Well, okay. Just be careful, please!"

Chapter Six

CRASH AND BURN

Chloe, Mateo, and Valeria stood at the top of Long Street. It was the perfect spot for a first downhill. It didn't have much traffic, it wasn't too steep, and if you got going too fast, you could easily bail on the grass next to the road.

Valeria stared down the street. She had ridden this road hundreds of times before. *I could probably do this blindfolded,* she thought. *So why am I so nervous?*

Mateo took the lead. "I'll go first," he said, "and then Valeria can tell you what I'm doing. I'll show you how to bail — that way if you get going too fast, you'll know what to do."

Mateo pushed off and started picking up speed. He carved a turn or two. After he got going a little faster, he jumped off his board into the grass.

"You don't need to carve right now," said Valeria. "Just start going down the hill a little bit, then bail. Make sure when you jump off your board, you really jump off and start running — like Mateo did."

"Got it," said Chloe. "I watched lots of videos last night. If I watch other people doing things a bunch of times, my body seems to know what to do — well at least it's like that for tennis."

Valeria understood. She loved watching videos of Ana Torres, her favorite pro rider. After she watched something enough, she could picture herself doing it too.

Chloe pushed off and scrunched low. As soon as she picked up speed, she jumped off the board and started running. Mateo and Chloe went down the hill a few more times. Each time, Chloe seemed to get more confident and even started carving a bit. Valeria filmed some of the runs on Mateo's phone so Chloe could watch herself later.

"*Qué padre!*" Mateo exclaimed after they watched a few.

"Um . . ." said Chloe. "What father?"

"It means, 'that's tight'!" said Mateo.

"Oh good," said Chloe. "I thought you were saying I longboarded like an old guy."

"Hey, Valeria," said Mateo. "It's your turn. Show Chloe how it's really done."

Valeria took a big breath. *This is nothing*, she told herself.

She stepped on her board, pushed off, and carved down the hill. She felt great as she began picking up speed. But in a flash, something caught her eye.

Her balance wavered. It shouldn't have been a big deal. But she panicked. Fear took ahold of her and she fell. Hard.

Chloe and Mateo ran toward her.

Valeria was not okay. She was embarrassed and confused. *How could I have fallen on such an easy hill?* she thought.

Chapter Seven

BRUISED EGO

The next day was awful. Valeria couldn't stop thinking about falling. She couldn't concentrate on her schoolwork. Mateo and Chloe tried to sit with her at lunch, but Valeria told them she wanted to be alone.

Later, in English, Mateo kicked Valeria's seat. "Hey," he whispered. "You okay?"

"I'm fine," Valeria mumbled.

"Wanna come riding after school?" he asked. "I'm trying to talk Chloe into doing the comp. I think she could handle it."

"Good for her," said Valeria.

"So, can you come?" Mateo pressed.

Valeria wished she had a real excuse. But she didn't. So she made one up. "I told Señora Cruz I'd help her again," Valeria said. "She's got lots of extra kids today."

"Okay, maybe tomorrow?" Mateo asked.

"Maybe," said Valeria.

After school, Valeria slumped down on the couch. Emilio came out of the bathroom, drying his hair with a towel.

"What're you doing here?" he asked. "I thought you'd be practicing for the comp."

"Nope," said Valeria, wishing she could explain everything to Emilio.

A few minutes later, Emilio came out of his room, ready for work.

"Can you come to the shop with me today?" he asked. "A big order came in and I could use your help."

Valeria shrugged. She often helped Emilio at the shop, but she wasn't sure she felt like going today. *Then again*, she thought, *it's not like there's anything to do around here all afternoon.* She peeled herself off the couch.

"It's settled then," said Emilio. "C'mon."

At the shop, Valeria unpacked boxes of bearings, decks, and wheels.

"Those ones are nice," said Emilio, nodding as Valeria pulled out a box of wheels. "They're awesome for riding in rainy conditions."

"Cool," said Valeria. She only had one set of all-purpose wheels. They were fine most of the time, but if the roads got wet, slipping became a major problem.

The door jingled as a man and a woman walked in.

Emilio jumped up. "Can I help you?"

The guy — in his forties, wearing a boarding T-shirt — smiled. "I'm Ned Turner," he said. "I'm running the downhill comp this weekend — have you heard about it?"

Emilio nodded to the event poster on the wall. "Of course," he said. "We can't wait."

"Cool," said Ned. "I wonder if you could help me out. Some of my people got delayed in New Zealand. Do you know some locals who could help set up hay bales and flags for the course?"

Valeria hardly noticed the conversation between Emilio and Ned. She couldn't stop staring at the woman who had entered with Ned and was now checking out the helmets by the door. It was Ana Torres!

Valeria walked over to Ana. "Hi, um, can I help you find anything?" she asked.

"Hi," said Ana. "Actually, I need some rain wheels. I forgot mine in New Zealand."

"Sure. They're over here," said Valeria. "I just unpacked some new ones."

They walked over to the counter. Valeria took a deep breath. She couldn't believe she was helping Ana Torres! "Why were you in New Zealand?" she asked.

"For the World Longboarding Championship," Ana said.

Duh! thought Valeria. *I knew that. I've been so wrapped up in my own head, I haven't even been watching comp clips the last few weeks.*

"Cool. How did you do?" Valeria was sure Ana had won. Ana Torres *always* won.

Ana shook her head and rolled her eyes. "I crashed and burned big time."

"Oh," said Valeria, surprised.

"It's okay," said Ana. "It happens! I lost my focus and tried to cut a corner too sharply. I ended up getting fourth. Kylie Jenkins won. It's all good."

Valeria pulled out two different sets of rain wheels from behind the counter.

Ana picked the yellow ones. "These are perfect." She paused, then looked at Valeria. "Hey, do you board?" she asked.

"Um, yeah," Valeria said. "I mean, I did, but then I broke my wrist. I went out the other day and crashed. I think I lost it." She looked at the floor.

"I totally get it," said Ana. "I've been there many times."

"Really?" asked Valeria. "Like you thought maybe you should quit?"

Ana laughed. "Well, yeah. I think we all feel that way about things we do. Pressure to live up to what we used to be, injuries, new people coming up the ranks who seem really good — you name it."

Just then, Emilio and Ned came over.

"You're making my baby sister's day!" said Emilio. "You're her idol."

Valeria blushed.

"Did she tell you that she won the U14 girls division the last two years?" he asked.

"Really?" said Ana. "That's impressive."

"Are you going to make it three years in a row?" asked Ned.

Valeria felt uncomfortable. "I haven't signed up yet."

Ana came to the rescue. "Why don't you help set up tomorrow?" she asked. "Scope out the course?"

Valeria jumped at the chance to be around Ana again. "That sounds great!" she said. *It doesn't mean I have to race*, she thought. *I can just help set up.*

"Fantastic!" said Ana. "Then I'll see you tomorrow."

Chapter Eight

HELPING ANA

"Are you ready?" asked Emilio the next morning. "I said we'd be there by eight."

Valeria headed for Emilio's car. *It's so cool I get to be around Ana today*, she thought.

"What, no board?" Emilio asked.

"No," said Valeria. "I'm just setting up."

"I'm sure Ana would sign it." he said.

Valeria hadn't thought of that. "I'll be right back," she said.

The whole road was blocked off for the event. There were probably a hundred people there. Some were throwing hay bales off a trailer. Others were hanging up banners or setting up vendor tents.

Ned already had Emilio's friends hard at work. They were lining the road with hay bales.

"Thanks for finding people. We couldn't do this without you." Ned said. Then he held up a bag. "Just a little thank-you — T-shirts for you and your friends. They're signed by all the Pro Tour boarders."

"*Chido*! Thanks," said Emilio, throwing Valeria a T-shirt. She put it on right away.

Ned turned to Valeria. "Ana said she needed help in the pro tent. She asked me to send you over when you got here. Are you cool with that?"

Valeria found Ana sitting in the tent. She had a stack of posters in front of her.

"Valeria!" she said. "I was hoping you'd come. I need help! They want me to sign all of these posters, then put one into each bag for tomorrow."

"What are they for?" asked Valeria.

"Swag bags for competitors," said Ana. "So far the bags have a water bottle and a sports bar. The featured pro at each comp has to sign the poster — and today, that's me. I was thinking I could sign them, and you could put them in the bags. That way it will go a little faster."

"Sure," said Valeria. "No problem."

About an hour later they were done.

"Cool," said Ana. "Let's go see if the course is ready. I want to take a look."

Valeria nodded.

"How about you? Are you going to race?" Ana asked.

"I haven't decided yet," said Valeria.

"Let's see how many people are signed up for your division," said Ana.

Ana pulled out her phone. "Well, there are only four girls signed up for your division. Haley Bennett, Chloe Platter, Eva Mendoza, and Lucy Mendoza."

"Chloe?" said Valeria.

"Do you know her?" asked Ana.

"Yeah," said Valeria. "She's pretty new. I guess she'll just have to take it slow."

Valeria knew the other girls too. They were serious local boarders from the next town over. They were always at the comps.

Haley and Eva worked hard, but Valeria had always beaten them in the past. Lucy was good, though. Really good. She had nearly taken first place from Valeria in last year's race. Just hearing their names sent a burst of adrenalin through Valeria.

"How about we sign you up?" said Ana.

Valeria couldn't believe it, but she was starting to feel excited.

Chapter Nine

COMP MORNING

"Valeria!" called Emilio. "You up?"

Valeria was up. In fact, she had been up for hours going over the course in her head. She always did that on comp day.

"Valeria!" Emilio shouted. "*Llegamos!*"

Valeria shoved everything she needed into her backpack and grabbed her board. On her way out the door, Coco handed her a canned protein smoothie.

"Good luck, *mi gatita!*" she said. "I wish I could be there to watch today, but Emily called in sick and I have to do her rooms."

"It's okay," said Valeria as she stuffed the can into her backpack. "I understand." She kissed her mom on the cheek, then followed Emilio to the car.

"Are *you* ready for today?" asked Valeria.

Emilio looked up at the cloudy sky. "Well," he said, "I think so. I might have to change my wheels if it rains."

Valeria followed Emilio's gaze to the cloudy sky. She didn't have rain wheels. If it rained, she would not be able to compete.

The pros were warming up when Valeria and Emilio arrived. Valeria found Mateo and . . . a girl dressed up like a gorilla.

"Chloe?" Valeria asked.

Chloe ripped off the gorilla mask. Under that mask was another — a hockey mask. "My mom's *making* me wear it." Chloe groaned. "But I'm gonna be a gorilla in protest! That way when people ask, 'Which one is your daughter?' she'll have to tell them, 'The one in the gorilla suit.'" Chloe grinned. "So what do you think? Pink or purple tutu to go with . . . hold on a sec —"

Chloe faced where spectators were gathering, then put on her gorilla mask. She began waving to her mom. Chloe's mom looked confused, then horrified.

"Purple," said Mateo. "Hey, you guys had better go. They're calling your group for course inspection."

After a brief safety meeting, the five U14 girls were allowed to inspect the 1.2-mile course. Inspection gave riders a chance to check out the full course up close — stuff like the curves and the road conditions — before riding it at race speed.

Valeria went slowly with Chloe. Maybe people thought she was just being nice, but Valeria was happy to go extra slow. And the longer she was on her board, the better she felt. Meanwhile, Chloe was riding like a natural. She fell twice on the corners, but was able to get back up quickly.

"Squat low and lean into the curves," said Valeria. "You're doing great!"

"Thanks," said Chloe. "One bonus to this suit — extra padding when I fall!"

The rain started just as the Women's Pro event began. The judges ducked under a tent, and the pros ran off to change their wheels. Valeria knew the comp wouldn't be canceled unless there was thunder.

Twenty minutes later, the rain had slowed to a sprinkle. The announcer told the boarders to line up. Big screens flashed on and Valeria found Ana in the lineup.

Soon they were off. Ana was off to a great start. Valeria cheered.

Chloe poked her, "Um, should I switch my wheels now?"

Wheels! Valeria had forgotten about her rain wheels problem . . . even if the rain stopped, the road would still be wet.

The crowd let out a groan and Valeria looked up — two of the racers had collided. Valeria looked for Ana. Then she heard cheering. Ana had won!

Chloe poked her again.

"Change them now," said Valeria.

As she showed Chloe how to swap out her wheels, her disappointment sunk in. *Too bad I can't conjure up a set of rain wheels out of thin air,* she thought.

Chapter Ten

A WINNER

Valeria was getting a drink of water when the athlete shuttle arrived, bringing the racers back up to the starting area.

"Valeria!" called Ana.

Valeria pointed to the medal around Ana's neck. "Congrats!" she said.

"Thanks," said Ana. "It's a fun course. A little slippery — but I'm sure you can handle it. Shouldn't you be getting ready?"

"I'm going to cheer, but I can't race," said Valeria. "I don't have rain wheels."

Ana ran over to the tool station and started taking the wheels off her board.

"Here," she said. "This set you sold me worked *great* today. They have a good vibe. I want you to use them."

"Really?" asked Valeria.

"Really," said Ana. "Just get out there and have fun. That's what it is all about. Don't worry about winning. Just have fun."

"Thanks!" said Valeria, smiling.

Valeria found Chloe and helped her finish tightening her wheels. Then she began putting Ana's rain wheels on her board as Emilio's group, the local U18s, raced. Emilio cruised into a third-place finish as she gave her board a final check.

"Emilio will be psyched with that!" Valeria told Chloe.

Just then the announcer called, "U14 girls to the starting area!"

There were a lot of laughs when Chloe the gorilla lined up. It helped loosen Valeria up. *Here goes!* she thought.

"Good luck, Chloe," said Valeria.

"You too!" said the gorilla.

Then they were off! The racers pushed off, trying to get as much speed as possible before the first steep downhill.

Valeria raced out ahead. She felt awesome! The wheels responded well and her body seemed to know just what to do. At the first steep downhill, she leaned forward with her hands clasped behind her back and got into a speed tuck.

This is so fun! she thought. The course was even better than she remembered. She began to get into a groove.

Suddenly, out of the corner of her eye, she saw the two Mendoza girls crash into one another! She hoped they were okay.

Just as she was trying to find her groove again, a flash of brown caught her eye. A dog had run onto the course. Valeria almost lost it, but she made a quick move to avoid the dog. Haley's attempt to dodge the dog brought her too close to the curb. She ditched, rolling off her board into the grass.

Just Chloe and me! thought Valeria.

Suddenly, Valeria lost her balance. She wobbled on the board and fell. Her board went rolling down the hill. She raced after it, finally grabbing it just before it toppled over a steep section.

As she ran back to the road, a blur of gorilla fur passed her. Chloe!

Valeria got back on her board. She tried to catch Chloe, but Chloe was really flying. As they entered the final stretch, Valeria was gaining on Chloe, but it was not enough. Chloe raced over the finish line a second in front of Valeria.

"Gorilla Girl wins!" said the announcer.

"Congratulations, Gorilla Girl!" shouted Valeria, hugging Chloe as they got off their boards at the finish area. Valeria felt great. She couldn't stop smiling.

"I can't believe it!" said Chloe. "I really won? I thought we tied. My extra gorilla suit weight must have given me an edge!"

Valeria was happy for Chloe. And she couldn't believe how happy she was with second place. Not only had she finally raced again, but she had owned that course. Even with the fall, she knew it was one of the best runs she'd ever had.

Just then, the announcer yelled. Mateo's group was starting.

The girls moved off the course. *It's funny,* Valeria thought as she and Chloe began clapping and yelling. *In a way, getting second place today feels more important than all of my first-place wins. I never would have expected that!*

She smiled, thinking about how strange life could be sometimes. Then she patted Chloe on the back and whooped as loud as she could. She hoped they could cheer Mateo on to a first-place finish.

AUTHOR BIO

Cari Meister has written more than 200 books for children. She lives in Colorado with her husband, four sons, a dog named Koki, and an Arabian horse named Sir William. She loves to visit schools and libraries. Find out more at *carimeister.com*.

ILLUSTRATOR BIO

Katie Wood fell in love with drawing when she was very small. Since graduating from Loughborough University School of Art and Design in 2004, she has been living her dream working as a freelance illustrator. From her studio in Leicester, England, she creates bright and lively illustrations for books and magazines all over the world.

SPANISH PHRASE GUIDE

chido (CHEE-doh) — cool

gatita (gah-TEE-tah) — little kitten

llegamos (yea-GAH-mos) — let's go

lo siento (LOW see-EN-toh) — I'm sorry

qué padre (KAY PAH-dray) — that's tight

GLOSSARY

adopt (uh-DAHPT) — the act of making a child a legal part of a family

adrenalin (uh-DREH-nuh-luhn) — a chemical the body produces when a person is excited

passion (PASH-uhn) — a very strong feeling, such as anger, love, or hatred

vendor (VEN-dur) — a person who sells something

DISCUSSION QUESTIONS

1. Talk about how Valeria felt about her accident. How did she feel before her cast was removed? How did she feel after competing in the comp? If her feelings were different, what caused the change?

2. Do you think Valeria was right to lie to Mateo by making up excuses to avoid going skating? Discuss your opinion.

3. Even though Valeria didn't win first place at the comp, she still felt happy about her performance. Talk about why she felt that way. How would you have felt in her position?

WRITING PROMPTS

1. In this book, Valeria, Mateo, and Chloe are friends who also longboard together. What do you and your best friends do together? Write about your favorite thing to do with your friends.

2. Although Valeria wasn't sure about racing, by the end of the story she was happy with her decision. Have you ever done something you felt nervous about at first but were later glad you did? Write two to three paragraphs comparing your experience to Valeria's.

3. Chloe showed a lot of confidence in finding friends at her new school. Make a list of ways you would make new friends if you moved.

MORE ABOUT LONGBOARDING

Can't wait to hit the nearest downhill?
Here's what you'll need. Local skate shops
can be very helpful if you have questions.

Deck

This is the wood board that you stand
on. There are many shapes and sizes
depending on whether you want to focus
on downhill, cruising, or slalom.

Trucks

These are the T-shaped metal pieces that
attach to the wheels.

Wheels

Which wheels you need depends on how
you plan to use your board and what kind
of riding you will do.

Bearings

Bearings are the round metal pieces that go inside skateboard wheels. There are a wide variety of bearings — they vary in cost and effectiveness.

Grip Tape

This is the sandpaper-like tape that you stick on your board. It helps your feet stay put. There are different kinds and colors.

Helmet, Slide Gloves, and Kneepads

Everyone crashes at some point. That makes these safety items essential. Always wear a helmet and kneepads. A slide glove has a hard plastic part on the palm. In longboarding, you often have to put your hand on the ground when you slide. No gloves equals bloody, ripped-up hands.

GIRLS with GAME

READ MORE
JAKE MADDOX
STORIES!

JAKE MADDOX

Pool PANIC

JAKE MADDOX

SQUAD STRUGGLES

JAKE MADDOX

SOCCER Show-Off

JAKE MADDOX

REBOUND TIME

JAKE MADDOX

VOLLEYBALL VICTORY

JAKE MADDOX

SOFTBALL Surprise

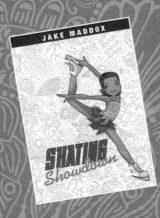

JAKE MADDOX

SKATING Showdown

JAKE MADDOX

Dancing Solo

JAKE MADDOX

Running SCARED

THE FUN DOESN'T STOP HERE!

Discover more:

VIDEOS & CONTESTS
GAMES & PUZZLES
HEROES & VILLAINS
AUTHORS & ILLUSTRATORS

www.capstonekids.com

Find cool websites and more books just like this one at **www.facthound.com**.

Just type in the book I.D.

9781496549723

and you're ready to go!